CHOOSE YOUR OWN ADVENTURE®
titles in Large-Print Editions:

YOU ARE A MILLIONAIRE

BY JAY LEIBOLD

ILLUSTRATED BY RON WING

An R.A. Montgomery Book

Gareth Stevens Publishing
MILWAUKEE

For a free color catalog describing Gareth Stevens' list of high-quality books, call 1-800-542-2595 (USA) or 1-800-461-9120 (Canada). Gareth Stevens' Fax: (414) 225-0377.

Library of Congress Cataloging-in-Publication Data available upon request from publisher. Fax: (414) 225-0377 for the attention of the Publishing Records Department.

ISBN 0-8368-1313-8

This edition first published in 1995 by
Gareth Stevens Publishing
1555 North RiverCenter Drive, Suite 201
Milwaukee, Wisconsin 53212 USA

CHOOSE YOUR OWN ADVENTURE® is a trademark of Bantam Doubleday Dell Books for Young Readers, a division of Bantam Doubleday Dell Publishing Group, Inc.

Original conception of Edward Packard.
Interior illustrations by Ron Wing. Cover art by David Mattingly.

1 2 3 4 5 6 7 8 9 99 98 97 96 95

Printed in the United States of America

YOU ARE A MILLIONAIRE

WARNING!!!

Do not read this book straight through from beginning to end. These pages contain many different adventures that you may have when you find a satchel filled with over a million dollars. From time to time as you read along, you will be asked to make a choice. Your choice may lead to success or disaster!

The adventures you have are the results of your choices. You are responsible because you choose! After you make a choice, follow the instructions to see what happens to you next.

Think carefully before you make a decision. Having a million dollars can be exciting—but being a millionaire can also be dangerous. Even if you are able to take the money home, you may not get the chance to spend it!

Good luck!

You're kicking around in a vacant lot with your friend Bruce. It's a hot summer day, your shirt is sticking to your back, and you're bored.

"Yo, amigo," Bruce calls to you. "Catch."

Bruce throws a ball from the other end of the lot, and you watch as it sails over your head and into a thicket of bushes. You sigh, and think maybe you should go home. You and Bruce have already played all the games you can think of, and he's beaten you every time. You're starting to get tired of him.

Bruce is all right to hang out with—until you run out of things to do. Then he starts getting bossy and tries to push you around. He likes to be in charge, and since he's bigger than you and your friends, he usually gets away with it. Still, you don't mind doing stuff with him, especially since your other friends are away at camp. Usually Bruce will shape up if you threaten to go home.

Besides, it's not all his fault. He doesn't like to talk about it, but there are a lot of problems in his family. He's even tried to run away a couple of times. And he doesn't have many friends. He knows he's a little funny looking, with his bristly black crew cut and his overgrown bulk and awkward limbs. But every once in a while, he surprises you. He's a bit of a daredevil, and sometimes he comes up with really good ideas.

"Okay, Bruce," you call to him, "go get the ball."

"No way," he calls back. "You missed it. You go get it."

Turn to page 2.

2

Time to go home, you say to yourself. You pull aside the branches and make your way into the bushes, trying to get a glimpse of the ball.

The problem is, you don't particularly like going home, now that Mrs. Harkley is there. Theresa, your younger sister, calls her "the horrible Mrs. Harkley."

At first you were excited when your parents said they needed some time alone and were going to spend the summer in Europe. But you groaned when you found out Mrs. Harkley would be staying with you. You asked if they could get someone else, but your mother said she wouldn't be able to find another person she could trust on such short notice. Besides, Mrs. Harkley was lonely and could use the work.

Go on to the next page.

She's mostly just weird—like the way she walks around the house with rubber bands on her wrist, as if she's going to shoot them at you if she catches you doing something wrong.

You do feel safe with Mrs. Harkley, and she does seem responsible. But instead of having more fun while your parents are gone, you have less. She makes you go to bed early. In the morning, after breakfast, she kicks you out of the house so she can sit around and watch soap operas all day. She doesn't like your friends to come over, and instead of chicken pot pies or spaghetti for dinner, you have to eat things she likes, like liver and okra. She even keeps the cookies hidden, doling them out one by one, and won't let you take food into the living room while you watch TV.

Go on to the next page.

Now, in the vacant lot with Bruce, you can't see the ball in the bushes and realize you'll have to go farther in to find it. You part the branches and plunge in. Your legs get scratched, and spiderwebs get in your face.

The ball is nowhere in sight. But something else catches your eye. It's partially buried under some twigs and leaves, as if hastily hidden. You brush aside the leaves and find an old beat-up leather satchel. It looks as though it's been through a war.

The satchel is heavy. You start to say something to Bruce as you unhook the clasp and open it up, but you stop dead when you look in. Your eyes bug open wide. "Holy moly," you whisper. "It's full of money!"

"Hey," Bruce calls, "what're you doing in there?"

You stop gaping at the money and watch through the branches as Bruce walks toward you. Should you tell him about it? Or should you hide the satchel and come back for it later?

You close the bag, thinking fast. Bruce is getting closer—he may already have seen you with it.

If you tell Bruce about the money, turn to page 75.

If you decide not to mention the money, turn to page 10.

6

Bruce lets up and gets to his feet. "That's right," he says with disgust. You stay on the ground, pretending you can't get up—which isn't far from the truth.

"Don't mess with me," Bruce says, strutting away. "That's all I'm telling you, don't mess with me."

"Right, Bruce," you mutter. Your lip is wet. Tasting, you realize it's blood.

"I hope you learned your lesson, twerp," Bruce taunts as he walks off.

"Jerk," you call after him.

"Wimp," he calls back.

"Donut!"

"Turkey!"

"Clod!"

"Dweeb!"

You keep up the the name-calling until Bruce's voice fades in the distance.

Turn to page 102.

You get up, stuff some hundred-dollar bills into your pocket, and eat a quick breakfast. Then, before Mrs. Harkley has a chance to ask you where you're going, you get out of the house and catch a taxi downtown to the shopping mall.

Your first stop is the electronics store. A salesman asks if he can help you. "I'm interested in a portable cassette deck," you say in a casual voice. "Top of the line."

The salesman shows you various tape boxes and explains their features. You choose one and add for good measure, "I'd like to get a Walkman, too." You're pleased by how polite and respectful the salesman is toward you. He seems to be begging you to buy more. "Not today," you say, "but maybe tomorrow." You peel off a few bills and march out of the store with your purchases.

Turn to page 19.

"Okay, I'll split it," you say resignedly. "If you can live with your conscience, that's your problem."

Bruce smirks. "That's right, and it's no problem."

You go to Bruce's house and divide the money. Even half of it is more than you can imagine what to do with. Having your hands on the money, you're tempted to keep it. But you remember your

words to Bruce and go straight to the police station before you have a chance to change your mind.

The sergeant who receives you gawks at the money when you show it to her. Then she becomes very suspicious and says, "Are you sure this is all of it?"

Turn to page 15.

"The ball's lost," you call to Bruce from the bushes.

"No, it's not," he says. "I'll find it. What's in there, anyway? I saw you pick something up."

"Nothing," you say, starting to make your way out.

"What?" he says, crashing his way in. "What is it?"

"Nothing," you repeat. You block his path. "Let's go get some ice cream."

"What's in here?" he insists. "Get out of my way."

For some reason, Bruce is set on looking around in the bushes. Maybe your tone of voice gave you away.

"Come on, Bruce, I'm tired of this," you say in an exaggerated voice.

You start to turn him around and push him back the other way. "Hey, get your grubby hands *off* of me," he says, knocking you aside.

Bruce seems determined. You try desperately to think of a way to stop him. All you can come up with is to call him a name and start a fight. You're sure to lose, but it might be the only way to keep him from finding the money.

_____

If you start a fight with Bruce,
turn to page 116.

If you resign yourself to letting him look in the
bushes, turn to page 91.

As Mustafa leads you out of the building, he looks at you strangely. Then he starts asking questions about what you saw in the vault. His English is not very good, and you think he must be angling for some money of his own. But he waves off your hand when you reach into the satchel.

"No *baksheesh*," Mustafa says. "I say this for you. I see something on your face. It happens, sometimes, to people who go into the tombs."

"What do you mean?" Bruce asks slowly.

Mustafa looks at the satchel. "You know, family of mummy give mummy all riches and wealth so he will have safe journey. If they don't give this, mummy's spirit will not be happy."

"We have to give something to the mummy?" you ask.

Mustafa shakes his head impatiently. "No, not to mummy. But like that, like mummy's family gives."

Bruce looks at him suspiciously. Mustafa just shrugs and says, "I don't say it for me. For you, for good health." He taps his temple. "I see things maybe you don't. I tell you what I see. That's all. You do what you want."

You reach the door. Mustafa gestures out at the street before you. "The world is big, we are small. Good-bye, my friends, and good luck."

"Good-bye," you say. As you realize that Mustafa was trying to help, you turn and call back, "Thanks."

Turn to page 29.

12

You grab the satchel full of money and lug it down the street. The bank is several blocks away, and by the time you heave the leather bag up to the teller's window, you're covered with sweat.

"May I help you?" the teller asks politely.

"I'd like to open a new account," you say in a businesslike voice.

"How much do you have to deposit?" she asks.

"I'm not sure," you reply, scratching your head. "About a million dollars, I think."

She smiles at you as she opens the satchel, but her face falls when she sees the money. She looks you over, and suddenly you're aware of your torn clothes, the blood on your face, and the bruises on your arms. "Is this *your* money?" she asks.

"Yes," you say confidently.

She makes some sort of movement with her foot, as if she's stepping on a bug. "Well then," she says smoothly, "would you like to put it in a checking account or a savings account?"

You're mulling over the advantages of each when suddenly you find yourself surrounded by men in blue uniforms. One of them puts a hand on your shoulder. Another grabs the satchel and says, "You'll have to come down to the station with us."

At the station, the police fill out forms and fingerprint you. Then a detective takes you into an interrogation room.

"Where did you get the money?" he asks.

Turn to page 94.

14

You grab the satchel and lug it down the street toward your house, hoping no one sees you. With your torn clothes and bloody face, you must be a real sight.

You go to the front door of the house, figuring Mrs. Harkley will be back in the kitchen making dinner. You turn the knob, slowly push open the door, and listen. All is quiet. Quickly you slip through the door, haul the satchel up to your room, and stash it in the back of your closet.

With the satchel safely hidden, you go down the hall and run a hot bath. Mrs. Harkley yells something up to you when she hears the water. "I'm taking a bath," you yell back.

You turn off the water, lock the bathroom door, and ease yourself into the hot tub. For a while you just lie and soak. You let your mind go blank, your scratches and bruises throbbing as the steam rises out of the water.

Once you feel like yourself again, you start to think about the satchel. Where did the money come from, and why did someone leave it in the bushes? Maybe they were being chased and had to hide it. But why?

Turn to page 20.

You have to admit to her that it's only half. And once she starts questioning you, you're unable to keep from telling her who has the other half. She immediately radios a patrol car to pick up Bruce.

The sergeant takes your name and address and tells you she'll be in touch with you about the money. "The final disposition," she says, "will depend on whether we can find the owner of the briefcase and what the source of the money is. But your friend, I'm afraid, is in a heap of trouble."

You never do hear from the sergeant, but months later you get a note from Bruce in detention hall. It reads, "You may be laughing now, but someday I'll have my revenge." You sit down right away to write your friend and try to convince him that you're not laughing at all.

The End

16

The corridor splits into a left- and right-hand turn. You go left, then suddenly run into what looks like an ordinary door.

"What do we do?" Bruce says.

You shrug. "What else can we do? Burst through the door as if we know what we're doing."

"You first," Bruce says.

You take a deep breath, grab the doorknob, and in one sharp motion swing it open and step through it.

You find yourself in an office with a desk and three startled members of the Egyptian Civil Guard. They gape at you for a moment, then quickly recover and grab you and Bruce.

"English?" the one seated behind the desk asks with arched eyebrows. He looks like an officer. He's got burnished skin, a thick black mustache, and handsome features.

"Er, yes," you stammer. "I mean, I'm American. But I speak English."

The officer smiles. "Ah, good." He motions for the guards to let you go. "Please sit down. Americans are our friends."

"Yes, we are good friends," you agree, searching desperately for something intelligent to say.

"America is a very great country," the officer goes on. "Very powerful, very rich."

Go on to the next page.

You wonder if he's hinting at something. Bruce seems to pick up on it, and he takes the satchel out of your hand. "That's right," he grins, "we're your rich friends, and we like to give presents to our friends."

You can see Bruce is about to pull some money out of the satchel. Is he being too brazen?

If you stop Bruce and take control yourself, turn to page 101.

If you let Bruce handle it, turn to page 95.

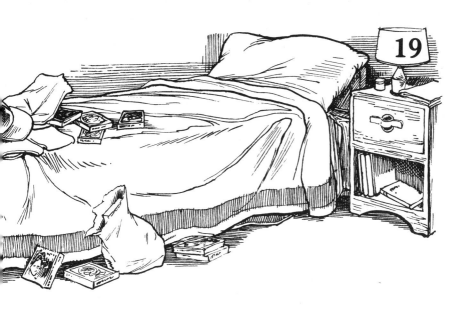

You decide you need something to play on your stereo, so you go down to the record store and buy some tapes you've always wanted. You spot a few more and buy them as well, just in case you get tired of the first ones.

That evening, Theresa discovers everything you bought. She's impressed with your tape player but doesn't think to ask how you paid for it. You play it for her, showing her how loud it can go. As you turn it back down, you can make out Mrs. Harkley's voice yelling something at you.

"Pipe down," you call back to her. Luckily she doesn't hear you.

The next day you decide you need a new bike, plus an aquarium, new clothes, and a VCR. The day after it's a computer, a leather jacket, and a fleet of radio-controlled cars.

Turn to page 40.

You picture the satchel sitting quietly in the darkness of your closet. There's something scary about it, like a bomb waiting to go off. Anything could happen.

You feel overwhelmed. Maybe you should tell an adult about it. Since your parents can't be reached in Europe, Mrs. Harkley is the logical person to tell. Even though she's weird, you should be able to trust her to know what to do.

Then again, you could take the satchel to the police. But what if the money belongs to some crook and the police don't know that when the crook comes to claim it? Or what if the police just decide to keep it for themselves? Aren't you just as good if not better a person to have it? Even if the money wasn't gotten dishonestly, you have to think that anyone carrying around cash like that must have hurt someone else to get it.

Mrs. Harkley's voice cuts through your thoughts. "Dinnertime!"

"I'll be down in a minute," you call back.

You set to work scrubbing the dirt and blood off your face as you try and decide what to do about the satchel.

If you tell Mrs. Harkley about the money, turn to page 50.

If you take the satchel to the police station tomorrow, turn to page 64.

If you keep the satchel for yourself, turn to page 109.

Once you've both settled down, you ask, "So how did you find out—"

"Well," Jean replies, "what happened was that a couple of captains saw that satchel full of money and they couldn't resist it. Once they realized they weren't going to find the owner, they began plotting to keep it for themselves. They tried to tie it up in red tape in a way that would allow the satchel to 'disappear.' But you know how these things work. More and more people had to be brought in on it, and finally someone spilled the beans."

"What about Sergeant Winooski?"

"She and a few other officers had an idea of what was happening and tried to stop it, but the two captains scared them out of probing any further. You saw how fast they transferred Winooski —and that was only one of the ways they threatened her. But don't worry. I have a hunch that when the dust settles, Winooski will be in for a promotion."

The next day Jean hands over the satchel to you, after counting out her ten percent. "I'll be able to take on a lot more deserving cases with this money," she says. She looks around the office and adds, "I'll also be able to move to a new building and hire a partner. What about you—what will you do with the money?"

You look down at the satchel and say, "I guess I'll have to think about that."

The End

Back in your room, you tell Theresa the whole story, from finding the satchel in the vacant lot to trying to keep it a secret. By the time you finish, she's jumping up and down on your bed. "Oh boy!" she says. "Think of all the things we can do. We can buy a horse!"

"Yeah, but there's one problem," you reply. "Where would we keep it? Besides, we can't let Mrs. Harkley or anyone else find out about the money or they'll take it away."

"Oh, that's right," she says. She sits down and thinks. "We need a hideout—someplace where we can do whatever we want."

"Like a castle, or a fort," you say.

"Hey, isn't there a fort in the woods?" Theresa asks. "You know, out behind the cable factory. Bruce and some guys have a fort back there."

"They do? Why didn't they tell me about it?"

"Everyone's got secrets," Theresa says. "I'll show you tomorrow."

In the morning, Theresa takes you out to the woods. The fort is a collection of cast-off wooden planks and railroad ties, cobbled together between four trees. It's on a secluded triangle of land, bounded by the river, the highway, and the back of the cable factory.

"It seems like you could do anything here and no one would know about it," you say.

Suddenly you hear voices behind you and the crackle of feet on leaves. As you turn, someone demands, "What do you think you're doing here?"

Turn to page 104.

On impulse, you thrust the satchel into Josef's hands. "It's yours," you say.

"Hey!" Bruce objects.

You hold up your hand to silence him. "Think about it, Bruce," you say. "Think about where the money came from, and what it was going to be used for. We've had our fun. Let's give it to someone who really needs it. Besides, they saved our lives."

Bruce looks down and mumbles, "You're right, I guess. But can we at least continue our trip?"

"That can be arranged," Josef says quickly. He pulls a few bundles of money out of the bag. "How much do you need?"

"That looks like enough," Bruce says, taking the bundles.

"Of course, you are both welcome to come to Mombawe as guests of honor," Nelson puts in.

"Not me," Bruce says. "I'm going to Greece."

But you feel differently. "I'd like to go to Mombawe," you say.

The helicopter lands, and you wish Bruce well as he heads off on his travels. You stay with Josef and Nelson, who take you back to Mombawe with them. You're so fascinated by what you learn there that you write home and ask permission to stay for another six months. You want to learn more and become involved in putting the money you found to use. Another year passes before you return home. By then, you've changed in ways you never could have imagined when you agreed to leave home with Bruce and travel.

The End

You tell Bill the whole story. He just shakes his head in amazement. "What are you going to do with it?" he asks.

"That's what I came to talk to you about," you reply. "But we can wait until later. Let's have some marshmallows and hang out for now."

The party gets wilder as the night goes on. You join in singing songs and telling stories. Then, as the flames begin to flicker, people start talking about what they want to do with their lives.

"I've got a question," Bill says. "What would you do if you had a million dollars?"

"I'd buy an island," a girl named Marina says. "With palm trees and warm, emerald-green water all around it. I wouldn't do anything but work on my tan."

"I'd put it away for college," a serious-looking girl named Ramona says. "It costs about that much these days."

"Who needs college when you have that much money?" a boy called Greg asks. "I'd invest it in the stock market and make a billion."

"Or lose it all," Bill puts in.

"Then I'd start taking over corporations," Greg goes on. "The first one I'd buy would be a candy company. Chocolate for life."

Turn to page 38.

The next day, you and Theresa meet Bruce, Kelly, and Roger at the fort. The five of you go down to the lumberyard to buy some wood for the clubhouse. Bruce is still skeptical, right up to the moment you put down the money at the cash register. But after that, he's convinced. You head for the hardware store to buy tools and then back to the fort to draw up plans for the house.

Every day for the next few weeks, you and Theresa tell Mrs. Harkley you're going to the swimming pool. She's glad to have you out of the house, so she doesn't ask questions.

More and more kids from the neighborhood join in your project. Each new person has a contribution to make, some new bit of knowledge or idea for improvement. The only thing you insist upon is that everyone is sworn to secrecy.

Every morning you get up and join the group in the woods to take measurements, saw boards, and hammer nails. Books from the library help you learn how to do it. Soon you have a spanking new clubhouse. Once the building and painting are done, you provide money for everyone to fill it up with whatever they want. The house becomes the scene of daily parties. Theresa starts building a stall for the horse she wants to get. Others begin work on all sorts of fascinating projects. You can't wait, each day, to find out what new things are going on at the clubhouse.

You can tell this is going to be the best summer you've ever had.

The End

28

An hour later, there's a tapping at the window. You open the door. It's Ramona and Lyla. "We have some work to do," Ramona whispers.

Bill sits up in his bunk. "What are you talking about?"

"We're not going to let the director get away with this, are we?" Lyla says. "We have to get the money back."

"We're in enough trouble," Greg grumbles.

"I can't believe you guys," Ramona says. "I thought you'd be up hatching a plot. You know what'll happen if we don't get the money back— the director will keep it for himself, and we'll be on KP for the rest of the month."

"What are you planning, some kind of commando raid on the director's office?" Bill asks.

"Exactly," Ramona says.

"Hey, I don't want to have a criminal record," Greg says. "Better we go on KP for a month and try to get the money back legally."

"But what if the director does notify the authorities and we can't get it back?" you ask.

"You don't understand," Ramona interrupts. "The director's going to keep it for himself, I know it, unless we do something."

"Forget it," Greg says. "I'm not going to be part of this."

Bill turns to you. "What do you think?"

If you want to make a commando raid on the office, turn to page 44.

If you decide to play it safe and wait, turn to page 45.

You and Bruce head straight for the airport to catch the first plane out of Cairo, which turns out to be a flight to Istanbul. As you wait in the boarding area, you ponder Mustafa's words. You don't feel as happy-go-lucky as when you got off the plane twenty-four hours ago. You have an inkling that the money you found may bring as much weight and responsibility with it as it does freedom and pleasure. You have plenty to think about as you continue your travels.

The End

True to his word, Bruce does not come back. Even the police can't find him. You keep the secret of the satchel to yourself and deposit most of the money Bruce left you in a separate account, using a little of it to buy a few things you've always wanted.

A few years later, you're walking down the street with your sister Theresa when a black limousine with darkened windows glides by. Suddenly it stops and waits for you to catch up. The window comes down, and a familiar voice calls, *"Yo, amigo!"*

You peer inside. "Bruce!" you say.

"The one and only," he replies with a big grin. "Get in."

You and Theresa join Bruce in the plush leather back of his limousine, fully equipped with telephone, television, and video games. He's decked out with an expensive haircut, tailored silk shirt, gold chains, and a Rolex watch.

"Wow," Theresa says, fingering the fine Corinthian leather. "Where'd you get all of this, Bruce?"

"Wise investments," he replies, winking at you. "Actually, I started up my own company. You know how it goes: the rich just keep getting richer. What can I say? I'm spoiled."

Turn to page 118.

Using the upstairs phone so that no one overhears you, you call a taxi and ask to be picked up at your corner. Then you throw some things into an overnight bag and get the satchel out of the closet—you don't want to risk Mrs. Harkley finding it. You write a note to Theresa telling her you've gone up to visit Bill and leave it on her bed.

You manage to slip out the front door with your bags. The cab is pulling up to the curb just as you arrive at the corner. You open the door, throw in the bags, and climb in. "Take me to Camp Pine," you say.

"In the mountains?" the driver says incredulously. "That's three hours away!"

You hand him a hundred-dollar bill from the satchel, saying, "I'll pay the rest when we get there."

As the cab heads into the mountains, you suddenly realize how crazy this trip is. But then you realize you *like* doing crazy things.

Three hours later, the taxi pulls up in front of the main lodge of Camp Pine. You pay the driver the rest of what you owe him, plus a big tip. "Thanks a lot!" he calls after you.

You find the camp director's office and ask the secretary where Bill is. She consults her activities sheet and tells you, "He's with the ditch-digging group."

"When will he be back?" you say.

"It's highly irregular to allow visitors," the secretary warns. "But if you stay out of the way, you can see him when he gets back tonight at seven."

Turn to page 61.

The next day you call Jean Fahey. "Yes," she says when you explain who you are, "Sergeant Winooski told me about the case. Why don't you come on down to my office?"

You ride your bike to a small storefront downtown. Jean Fahey isn't what you expect a lawyer to look like—she's a big-boned woman with a gentle face, and she's wearing blue jeans.

She has you tell her the whole story from the beginning. When you're finished she says, "It certainly sounds like something fishy is going on. But I can tell you right now, it's tough to recover anything from the police department. The normal procedures sometimes don't apply or don't work. I'll have to pull a few strings. I have a friend in the district attorney's office I can call, but if worse comes to worst, we may have to go to the press with this story. Do you think you can handle that?"

You nod.

"It's your decision," she continues. "Now, normally I charge an hourly fee. But in this case, I'd like to charge ten percent of whatever I recover for you. How does that sound?"

"That sounds fine," you say.

"I'll call you as soon as anything happens."

You leave Jean Fahey's office with the feeling that if anyone can get to the bottom of this, she can. You're not wrong. Two weeks later she calls to say, "The wheels are turning. The district attorney is making an investigation. There will be a hearing on Monday morning—are you ready to testify?"

"I'll be there," you say.

Turn to page 72.

34

You're nervous, but decide to trust your good feelings about the group. You tell them about the money you found, bringing out your satchel to prove it. "So I came up here to talk to Bill about what to do with it. I like your ideas," you add.

"Forget about those," Greg says. "If we're talking real money here, you should just deposit it in high-interest savings accounts and bonds."

"No," you reply. "I've decided I want to do something more exciting with it. Why not take a chance? I want to do a group project. You can be the investment advisor, Greg."

Greg raises his eyebrows and decides not to discourage you anymore. But Ramona speaks up. "Shouldn't you turn the money in to the police?"

A chorus of groans goes up from the circle. "They'll just keep it for themselves," someone says. "Or give it back to the swindler who lost it," someone else adds.

"What kind of group project do you have in mind?" Bill asks you.

"I'm not sure," you reply. "Something where everyone can do what they're good at."

"Like on my island," Marina says. "Lyla will have her television station, Ramona will start her wildlife refuge, Tom will have his telescope, Greg will manage the investments, and so on. And me, I'll be in charge of suntans."

"I think we should buy the camp," Bill says. "Then we could set up a really fun camp where kids could come and do all the things they really want to do."

Turn to page 54.

You keep breathing deeply and regularly, adding in a few snores for effect. As you hear your closet door open, the familiar smell of baby powder reaches your nostrils, and immediately you know who the intruder is.

"Mrs. Harkley!" you bark.

Mrs. Harkley screams and jumps. You switch on your lamp and say, "What are you doing?"

Mrs. Harkley squints and shields her eyes from the light. She's pale as a ghost. "I was just making sure—" she begins. "Actually, I just wanted to see it—the money," she explains, edging toward the door. "I was just so curious about what it looked like—I couldn't help myself. I'll phone the ad in first thing in the morning—good night," she mumbles, closing the door behind her.

You hide the satchel in a new place in your room before you come downstairs in the morning. Instead of being hunched over her newspaper with her coffee as usual, Mrs. Harkley is acting bright and cheery-eyed. She asks if you slept well and if she can fix you anything for breakfast—"Eggs? Pancakes? What would you like?"

You mutter that you'll get yourself a bowl of cereal and a Pop Tart. This doesn't dampen her mood, however. She tells you that she's phoned in the ad, and she's going to sit right there beside the telephone all day. You can tell you're not going to be able even to get close to the phone to talk to anyone who calls, so after you finish breakfast you get your suit and towel and go down to the local pool for a swim.

Turn to page 43.

36

At home, you explain to Theresa that you've been saving money for years and now you've decided to spend some. You know she knows you're not giving her the whole story, but you decide it's better not to bring her into it.

The next day, after Mrs. Harkley has gone shopping, you go out into the backyard with a shovel and dig a deep hole. You wrap the satchel in several plastic garbage bags, drop it in the hole, and quickly cover it over with dirt. You then hide the hole by putting dead leaves and grass over it.

Now that you've gotten rid of the money, you feel as though a weight has been lifted from your shoulders. You don't have to worry about being discovered. You don't have to worry about whom to share the money with. Instead, you can go on with your normal life, knowing that sometime in the future, when you need it, when you're ready for it, you'll be able to dig up your treasure.

The End

38

"I'd buy a baseball team," a freckly boy named Peter says. "Then I could be the manager."

"What a bunch of capitalists," Ramona says. "After I had enough for my education, I'd use the rest for a good cause."

"Yeah, you could start a wildlife refuge," someone says.

"Or find a cure for cancer."

"I'd like to feed all the hungry children in the world," Greg says in a mock-sweet voice. "For one day. Then they can go back to starving. I hate to tell you this, Ramona, but a million dollars isn't going to solve the world's problems."

"It's a start," Ramona replies. "You're just going to cause more. Your candy company will probably pollute the water and then make other people pay to clean it up."

Turn to page 53.

In the morning you're awakened by the insistent ringing of the doorbell. You throw on your bathrobe and tromp downstairs, passing a note on the way that says, "We've gone to the grocery store. Back soon. Love, Mrs. H."

You open the door to catch a man dressed in a khaki shirt, khaki pants, and aviator sunglasses in the act of pressing the doorbell again. "Oh, I didn't think anyone was home," he says with a start. His clear blue eyes appraise you from under a pair of bushy brows. "I came about the satchel," he adds.

"Can you describe it?"

"Well, it's tan-colored, beat-up leather, about so big," he says, drawing a rectangle in the air.

"Does it have any initials on it?"

"Yes," he says, exasperated, "but I don't know what they are. Your grandmother, or whoever she is, asked me that last night on the phone. I can't be bothered with details like that. But she didn't give me a second chance—she just cut me off."

You say nothing, wondering what to do. "Listen," he goes on, "I can tell you the most important thing about the satchel: it's full of money. I had to hide it in the bushes because I was being chased by foreign agents. Let me tell you what the money is for, and I think you'll agree that it should be returned to me."

You nod uncertainly, and the man comes into the living room. He removes his sunglasses, sits on the couch, and motions for you to do the same. "My name's Jack West," he says confidentially, "and I'm a special operative. You know, a spy."

Turn to page 56.

40

For the next week, shopping is the main activity in your life. Every day you get up, eat breakfast, and head down to the mall for a hard day of finding, appraising, and buying stuff.

The more you buy, the more you think of to buy. But strangely, the more you buy, the less satisfying each new item is. Not only that, it gets harder and harder to enjoy your new things. If you show too many of them to Theresa or your friends, they'll catch on to your secret.

Already people are asking questions like, "What'd you do, rob a bank?" You just laugh and change the subject. But you have to sneak more and more of your new purchases into the house and hide them away in your closet. You find yourself becoming secretive and paranoid.

Then one day at the mall, as you're plopping down a few hundred for a CD player, you feel a tug on your sleeve. It's Theresa, staring wide-eyed at the wad of bills in your hand.

"Wow," she breathes, "where'd that come from?"

"Oh, I've been saving it up," you say, as if it's no big deal. Theresa just looks at you.

Go on to the next page.

You realize it's time to make a decision. You can't keep piling things up in your closet unless you tell Theresa and your friends about the money—and maybe share it with them. Otherwise, you'll have to hide it, and hide it well. It almost seems like the money is more trouble than it's worth. Maybe you should just bury it. Then when you're older, you can dig it up and figure out what to do with it.

Theresa is still looking at you. "Wait until we get home," you say.

If you tell Theresa about the money, turn to page 23.

If you bury the money instead, turn to page 36.

When you come back for lunch, you find a man sitting at the kitchen table. "Did you come for the satchel?" you ask.

He laughs. "No," he says, casting a glance toward the door.

Mrs. Harkley comes into the room and introduces the man. "This is my nephew Roscoe."

Roscoe smiles at you, shakes your hand, and says heartily, "Pleased to meet you." He's about thirty years old, muscular, with short-cropped blond hair and a clean-scrubbed face. There's something about the way his skin shines that gives you the creeps.

"Roscoe used to be in law enforcement," Mrs. Harkley explains. "I thought—well, with all that money around, we shouldn't take any chances."

Roscoe winks at you, makes a pretend gun with his thumb and forefinger, and clicks his tongue as he pulls the trigger. "I also happen to know a little bit about money management," he says. "That is, just in case we don't find the owner."

You go to the cupboard and fix yourself a peanut butter and jelly sandwich. "I have contacts in the business world," Roscoe goes on. "There are a lot of things you could do with that money."

"I guess we'll worry about that when the time comes," you say, taking your sandwich into the living room to watch cartoons.

That evening, the telephone rings several times. You listen, and every time you overhear Mrs. Harkley say, "No, I'm sorry, that's not it."

When you go to bed, you lock your door, just to make sure.

Turn to page 39.

"Let's make a raid," you say.

"Good," Ramona says. She pulls you, Bill, and Lyla into a circle and begins plotting how to rescue the satchel. After a while Greg says, "Oh all right, I'll join you."

"Lucky us," Lyla murmurs.

Half an hour later, you set the plan in motion. Ramona and Lyla go back to their cabin, while you, Greg, and Bill put your most important belongings into your backpacks. You all meet by the creek behind the director's office, where you leave your packs. Greg and Bill head back toward the main lodge. Lyla goes up the creek toward the stables. You and Ramona wait in the shadows behind the office with a Swiss army knife, listening carefully.

Fifteen minutes later, you hear the distant sound of breaking glass. "Bill and Greg are in the kitchen," Ramona says. "Let's go."

You creep up to the back window of the director's office. The window is partially open but blocked by a screen. Ramona locks her hands in a stirrup. You step up and cut a square out of the screen with your knife. Then you push the window open and climb in.

You pull Ramona quickly inside, then you both turn on your flashlights and begin searching the office. You open every drawer and file, but there's no sign of the satchel.

Turn to page 67.

"I agree with Greg," you say. "Let's try to get the satchel back the legal way. Even if we manage to steal it back from the director, we might still get arrested. I think we should play it safe and wait."

"Wimps," Ramona grumbles.

"It's for the best," Greg says, putting his hand on her shoulder.

First thing in the morning, you call Mrs. Harkley to come pick you up. You ask her to take you straight to the police station where you file a complaint against the director.

The police promise they'll investigate. Soon charges are filed, and eventually the case comes to court. At the trial, the director claims that you, Bill, and his friends are making the whole thing up.

"They were engaged in illicit activities," he says. "They were out after curfew, having some kind of party around an illegal camp fire. There never was any satchel of money." He pauses, then goes on, "Obviously these kids are troublemakers, and they have it in for me. This is just another one of their stunts."

Despite the testimony of the rest of the people present at the campfire, the judge returns a verdict of not guilty. "I'm sorry," he says to you. "There just isn't enough evidence. It was your word against his." Turning to the director, the judge says, "You're a free man."

Soon after that the director leaves the camp and is never heard from again.

The End

You return to the station early the next morning. Sergeant Winooski's office is empty. Her desk is cleaned out, and the walls are bare. You check to make sure you have the right office, then ask a passing officer if Sergeant Winooski has moved.

"She got transferred," he says, not looking up from a clipboard he's reading.

"Where to?" you ask.

"How should I know?" the officer growls, and keeps walking.

Other policemen are no more helpful. Finally one of them says to you, "Look, kid, why don't you just get lost?"

You walk home from the station dejected. Obviously something is wrong. That night you manage to track Sergeant Winooski down in the phone book and call her at home. She sounds guarded when she recognizes your voice. "I'm sorry I disappeared on you," she says. "You have to understand, I'm on very thin ice right now. I'll tell you what you should do. Call a friend of mine. Her name's Jean Fahey, and she's a children's rights lawyer—"

"I'm not a child," you break in.

"Don't worry," Winooski responds. "She's good. Very good. She'll be able to help you a lot better than I can."

Go on to the next page.

You take down Jean Fahey's phone number and thank Sergeant Winooski, saying, "I appreciate your help."

"I wish I could do more." She sighs. "Good luck."

You look at the piece of paper with Jean Fahey's number on it. You're skeptical about calling her. You wonder if what you really need is a private investigator, someone tough who can find out what's really going on.

If you look for a private investigator, turn to page 80.

If you call Jean Fahey, turn to page 33.

You go back to your regular life, deciding that the money was more trouble than it was worth. For a while you receive quarterly dividends from Roscoe, along with a little report on his investments. You and Theresa each open an account and save the money for your education. Mrs. Harkley retires to Florida.

As time goes on, you hear less and less often from Roscoe. Eventually you hear nothing. You forget all about him—until one day, as you're walking downtown, you see a grizzled man you vaguely recognize. He asks you for a quarter. It's not until later in the day that you realize it was Roscoe.

The End

50

You dry off, dress, and go down to dinner. Mrs. Harkley has made another one of her meals—ground turkey, boiled turnips, and lima beans. You look at Theresa, who rolls her eyes, and start eating.

"So," Mrs. Harkley says, "what happened to you today?"

You decide to tell her the story of how you were kicking around the vacant lot with Bruce when you found the satchel in the bushes. As you speak, Theresa and Mrs. Harkley stare at you dumbfounded.

"So," you say after some silence, "I'm not sure what to do."

"You could buy a horse," Theresa says.

"You mean I could buy a horse for *you*," you reply.

"And a ranch, too," she adds.

"Why—why, yes," Mrs. Harkley says, finally finding her voice. "There are lots of things you could do with that kind of money—"

"But shouldn't I try to find out who lost it?" you ask.

"Oh—oh, yes, of course," she says quickly. "Absolutely. Why the poor person who lost it must be going out of their mind with—panic." She stops and thinks. "But then, if they were so careless as to leave it lying around in a vacant lot, maybe it doesn't mean very much to them."

Go on to the next page.

"Maybe they were being chased," you say.

"I suppose so," she says. "Which means that they may be . . ." Her voice trails off, and then she says, "You know, it may be very, very hard to find this person. I don't know how we're going to do it."

"We can advertise in the Lost and Found," Theresa puts in.

Mrs. Harkley lets out a burst of laughter. "Theresa, dear, you can't just run an ad that says, 'Found: A million dollars!'"

Turn to page 82.

Bruce's logic is hard to refute. "Then I guess we should take it to the police," you say.

"No way," Bruce counters. "That will only give the bad guy a chance to get it back. And if he doesn't, then the police will give it to the government, and they'll spend it on a nuclear bomb."

You still don't feel right about keeping the money. "Well, then," you say, "we should give it to some deserving people."

"Yeah," Bruce says, "like us."

You and Bruce stare at each other for a full minute. "Think about it," he says. "We can do anything we want. We can travel around the world."

"I guess if we do keep the money, it won't be very smart to hang around here," you say. "If the person who lost it catches us, they probably won't be very nice about it."

"Exactly," Bruce agrees. "Come on. Where do you want to go? It's up to you. We'll travel for a while, then decide what to do with the rest of it when we get back."

A vision of the pyramids of Egypt flashes through your head. Bruce's idea is tempting. Maybe you should stop worrying about what the right thing to do is and have some fun.

If you take Bruce up on his offer to travel, turn to page 83.

If you try to find the owner of the satchel instead, turn to page 113.

"I'd buy a huge telescope," a skinny boy named Tom puts in, "and a supercomputer. I'd be an independent scientist and spend all my time looking at the stars and making discoveries."

"Sounds real fun," Marina snorts. "But I'd let you put your telescope on my island."

"I'd buy a TV station and make programs for my friends, so we wouldn't have to watch regular television," a girl named Lyla says.

"You can have that on my island, too," Marina says.

"How about a summer camp?" Bill says. "So we don't have to do the dumb things they make us do here."

"Yeah, I'd buy Camp Pine, and on the first day I'd fire the director," Ramona says.

"What a great idea!" Bill says. He looks at you. "What do you think? It could be an investment."

Everyone looks at you with curiosity. If you're going to tell them about the money, now is obviously the time. But you're not sure. Do you want to share the money with this group? Or would you rather stay quiet and keep it to yourself?

If you decide to involve the group, turn to page 34.

If you'd rather not say anything about the money, turn to page 84.

54

Suddenly a huge shadow looms against the fire-lit trees. "The party's over," a booming male voice announces.

You look up to see the camp director. He strides into the circle and before you can react grabs the satchel, saying, "I'll have to confiscate this."

You and the rest of the group sit stunned around the fire. The director looks over the group sternly. "Frankly, I'm disappointed in you people," he says. "I thought you knew better than to pull a stunt like this."

You all troop back to camp, your heads hanging. When you reach the cabins, the director says, "We'll talk about disciplinary measures in the morning. For now, you're all confined to your bunks." Turning to you, he adds, "And you're out of here first thing tomorrow."

"That's my money—" you start to say.

"Quiet!" the director commands, clutching the satchel under his arm. "I know how you got this money. Once I notify the authorities, you'll be in big trouble."

You lie down in a borrowed sleeping bag on the floor of Bill's cabin. Bill and his friends try to console you. "Don't worry," Bill says. "He can't take the money away from you. We'll figure out a way to get it back in the morning."

But you can't get to sleep. You toss and turn, wondering whether you really will be able to get the money back.

Turn to page 28.

56

Jack West's manner suddenly changes, his voice becoming more authoritative. "You probably haven't heard of a country in Africa called Mombawe, but it was recently taken over by groups who, well, hold in contempt everything dear to us. These groups engineered an uprising that overthrew the ruler of Mombawe. This ruler had been very well-disposed toward the interests of our government, but he was replaced with what the revolutionaries call 'democracy.' Some concerned citizens in this country got together to support a movement to return the rightful ruler to power.

"I've been working with the freedom fighters there, and believe me, a braver lot of men you'll never see. All I can say is it's a shame they don't get more support. Luckily, though, our network helps them out. We arm them, advise them, even fight by their side. But what do we need most? Money.

"I'm making many sacrifices, but I don't ask for anything in return. I'm not worried about the honor, the glory, my own profit, anything like that. I just consider it my patriotic duty to help a small country in distress."

West fixes you with his blue eyes. "I worked hard to raise the money in that satchel. Now, will you be a patriot, too, and hand it over to me?"

You consider what West has said. It certainly sounds as if the satchel belongs to him. But you're not sure if you buy his story.

If you get the satchel, turn to page 63.

If you say you'll have to think about it, turn to page 92.

You clamber out the window and onto the ledge. West is running up the shingles of the sloped roof above you. You grab the gutter and hoist yourself onto the roof. Scrambling to the peak, you see West heading down the other side. Then a shriek comes from below, and you hear Mrs. Harkley scream, "There's a man on the roof! Roscoe, come quick!"

West straddles the top of a window gable and aims his gun at the driveway, waiting for Roscoe to appear. You take a second to gauge the distance. Then you spring off the ridge of the roof, slide down, and smash into West just as he pulls the trigger. The impact knocks him off the gable, and he slides over the edge with a scream. The satchel teeters for a moment, then follows him.

You peer over the edge to see Roscoe training a gun on West, who's lying on the ground. Theresa grabs the satchel and runs inside. "Good work, Theresa," Roscoe calls after her. "Put it in a safe place."

"My leg," West moans. "I think it's broken."

"You've got a lot more to worry about than that, my friend," Roscoe smirks. "Get me some rope," he directs Mrs. Harkley.

Mrs. Harkley rushes inside, and you start to climb down a tree next to the house. Before you reach the bottom, you hear sirens coming around the corner.

"Hey!" Roscoe cries. "Who called the cops?"

"I did," Theresa says from the doorway.

Turn to page 77.

58

You and Bruce jump back at first, but then move in for a closer look. The mummy is surprisingly small and frail. It almost looks as though it's made of mud, with its bones and facial expression frozen for centuries. You find something strangely touching about it. You can feel a little of the personality and spirit of this human who walked the earth five thousand years ago—and the sadness of its death.

"I wonder what else is in here," Bruce says, shining the flashlight around. A niche of some kind has been built into the wall, and another smaller mummy has been placed in it.

"It's a cat!" you exclaim. "Look, here are the ears, and the tail, all wrapped up."

"Weird," Bruce says. "They made their cats into mummies, too?"

The cat mummy is almost as touching as the human one, when you think about the care given to the little carcass. It gives you a vivid sense of the daily life of this person.

You find more niches around the chamber. One contains a dog, another a hawk. There are crocodiles, snakes, even a little mouse, all mummified. You also find plates, bowls, pitchers, and cups. Some of them contain hard, shriveled-up nodules of what was once food.

"Everything needed for the afterlife," you muse.

Go on to the next page.

You feel Bruce shiver beside you. "It gives me the creeps. All of a sudden I feel like I'm disturbing this dude's rest. You know all those stories about the mummy's curse? Let's get out of here."

"Yeah," you agree, "let's go."

You find a corridor leading out of the burial chamber and follow it through the cool, dusty passageways, feeling as if you've entered another universe.

Turn to page 16.

You spend the afternoon hanging around the camp. It doesn't look like a very fun place. When Bill arrives, tired but happy to see you, he confirms your impression. "This place is more like boot camp than a summer camp. They make us get up at six and do calisthenics. Then we all have chores, like scraping paint or cleaning the latrines. Even when we do get to do activities, they take all the fun out of it by making it into a big competitive thing."

Bill checks to make sure no counselors are listening before he goes on. "But stick around. A bunch of us are going to sneak out tonight and have a campfire in the woods. How'd you get up here, anyway?"

"I'll tell you tonight," you answer.

Later that night, you meet Bill and a bunch of other campers in a clearing in the woods. You recognize some of them from school, but even those you don't know seem friendly. You all set to work building a fire and collecting wood. Soon a bright blaze is burning, with everyone gathered around it, toasting marshmallows and telling stories.

"So," Bill says to you, "what are you doing here?"

Instead of answering, you pull him aside and open the satchel for him. It takes a moment for the contents to register with him, and then he draws in a sharp breath.

"What'd you do, rob a bank?" he whispers.

Turn to page 25.

62

Roscoe returns shortly, clutching the satchel. You, Theresa, and Mrs. Harkley greet him at the door. "Are you all right?" Mrs. Harkley asks.

"Not a scratch," he says with a wave of his hand. "But," he goes on, tapping his finger on the satchel, "I think I'd better take charge of this. It's obviously dangerous business. Besides, I've earned a share of it."

"Who was that man?" Theresa asks.

You explain how West came for the money and pulled the gun on you.

"Well," Roscoe says, "at least he's out of our hair now. The money's ours, free and clear. Now you just watch, with my financial knowledge, I'll double or triple it in a matter of months. And we'll all get our share."

"We'll be rich!" Mrs. Harkley declares gleefully. "We're set for life!"

"Shouldn't we tell the police?" Theresa asks.

Roscoe's eyes narrow. "Don't you dare," he growls.

"Don't worry, honey," Mrs. Harkley tells her. "You'll be glad you left it up to us."

"I'm off," Roscoe says with a salute. "It's time to put these greenbacks to work!"

Turn to page 49.

You run upstairs and get the satchel for Jack West. His face lights up when you hand it to him. He opens it to make sure all the money is there. Then he shakes your hand and says, "You're a shining example for right-thinking people everywhere." He hands you a hundred-dollar bill. "Here's a little reward."

West gives you a salute and marches out the door. You watch him disappear down the street, and a moment later Mrs. Harkley's car pulls into the driveway. You help carry in a bag of groceries. After you've set them on the counter, you say, "A man came for the satchel, and I gave it to him."

Mrs. Harkley looks stricken. She manages to choke out, "The whole thing? When?"

"Just now," you reply. "His name was Jack West. I'm sure it belonged to him. He said it was for some freedom fighters in—"

Before you can finish, Roscoe dashes out the door. Mrs. Harkley explodes at you, "You fool! Don't you know what we could have done with that money? We'd have been set for life! We were rich!"

All you can think of to say is, "But it didn't belong to us."

Turn to page 79.

64

The next morning you lug the satchel down to the police station. You tell the officer at the front desk that you want to turn in a lost briefcase, and he directs you down the hall to the office of a hearty woman who introduces herself as Sergeant Winooski.

"I found this in a vacant lot near my house," you tell the sergeant, heaving the satchel onto her desk. "I thought I'd better turn it in."

"Why, what's in there?" she asks.

"It looks like about a million dollars," you respond.

She smiles at you, pulls the satchel toward her, and opens it. Her smile changes to a look of amazement when she sees the money. She flips through a bundle of hundred-dollar bills and says, "You know, you just might be right."

Sergeant Winooski takes out some forms and starts asking you questions about how and where you found the satchel. When it's all done, she says, "We'll get on this right away." She looks at you and pauses before going on. "You know, not everyone would have been as honest as you, turning in the money. I respect that. And who knows, you just might get it back. If we can't find out where it came from in thirty days, it'll be yours."

You thank her and say good-bye.

"Bye," the sergeant says. "I'll be in touch."

You go home feeling as though you've done the right thing. You try not to think too hard about what kind of reward you'll get if the police do find the owner of the satchel—not to mention what will happen if they *don't*.

Turn to page 103.

The man in the khaki outfit gets off his horse and between gasps says, "That money belongs to the freedom fighters of Mombawe, not to you kids. Hand it over right now!"

"Let's go, Hamid!" you say, adding another note to his pile. Hamid revs the engine.

"Freeze!" the man yells. At that moment one of the camels, upset by his shout, makes a bellowing noise, bares its yellow teeth, and spits in the man's face. He falls to the ground, clutching at his eyes.

The jeep roars off, and you careen down the little dirt road. Hamid blares his horn at anyone who gets in the way. Farmers working in their fields, children herding goats, bicycles, carts, and donkeys carrying loads of hay scramble out of the way, staring as you speed by.

To your dismay, the man in the khaki outfit has commandeered a jeep, too, and is coming after you. Hamid takes a zigzag course over the tiny dirt roads of the fertile strip of farmland along the Nile, but he can't shake the man.

"What are we going to do?" Bruce yells to you.

"I don't know," you answer. "Maybe we can lose him in the desert."

"Felucca," Hamid says. He makes wave motions with his hand and gestures toward the Nile. "Like a sailboat."

"I can't swim," Bruce complains. You look at Hamid, but he just shrugs. On one side of you is the Nile, on the other the desert.

If you decide to take a felucca, turn to page 105.

If you go into the desert, turn to page 112.

"What if he put it in a safe?" you whisper to Ramona.

Before she can answer, a door slams on the other side of the building. You and Ramona switch off your flashlights and rush for the window. The director's voice booms from somewhere outside. "What's going on in there? *What is going on?!*"

"He's headed for the kitchen in the main lodge," Ramona says. "Let's go check his bedroom—if the satchel isn't there, we're done for."

You go through the secretary's office and across the hall to the door of the director's living quarters. You push it open very slowly and listen. All you hear is the distant sound of crashing plates and the irate voice of the director. You motion Ramona in.

You're in his private kitchenette. Light is coming from another room. As you head toward the light, an ominous growling comes from the corner. You run out of the kitchenette and into the bedroom, slamming the door behind you. A dog starts barking madly.

"Look!" Ramona exclaims. "It's on the chair!"

She grabs the satchel from underneath some clothes. "Let's get out of here!" you say.

You climb out the window and jump to the ground. As you turn to take the satchel from Ramona, the director comes running back from the lodge. "Stop!" he cries when he sees you. "Thieves!"

Go on to the next page.

Ramona jumps down, and together you race to the spot by the river where you left your packs. Lyla is waiting there with the horses. Bill and Greg, already mounted, rein their horses around to head off the director, who is yelling as he pounds after you. This gives you and Ramona a chance to jump onto your horses.

"Hiyo Silver, away!" Ramona cries, waving her hand forward. The five of you splash across the

creek and gallop away into the woods, leaving the director behind.

The only thing left for you to figure out is how to spend the money.

The End

70

In one swift motion you jump out of bed, grab the bat, and bean the burglar on the head. The body thunks heavily to the floor. You switch on a light, only to find you've just knocked out Mrs. Harkley!

You drop to your knees and put your ear to her mouth. Thankfully, she's still breathing. You run down to Theresa's room, crying, "I've just beaned Mrs. Harkley!"

Theresa sits up in bed, rubbing her eyes. "She wasn't *that* bad—"

"No, it was an accident!" you say. "I thought she was a burglar. I'd better call an ambulance."

Fifteen minutes later, a team of paramedics rushes in to take Mrs. Harkley away on a stretcher. You feel terrible about what you've done, but one of the medics tells you, "It looks like she'll pull through."

In the morning, you and Theresa ride your bikes to the hospital. The doctor tells you Mrs. Harkley has a concussion. "She's still under observation and can't see anyone yet. We'll have to keep her here for a while."

As you ride back home with Theresa, you start to think that maybe the money is a bad influence. You've already hurt one person. True, Mrs. Harkley brought it on herself. And there's no telling what she would have done with the money. But should you risk any more trouble? you wonder.

You resolve to take the money to the police first thing tomorrow.

Turn to page 64.

The next morning you and Bruce take the elevator up to the dining room, where you have a breakfast of eggs and *fuul*—a thick bean paste. Bruce takes you to the window and points to the southeast. Shimmering on the horizon above the chaotic city are three triangular shapes. "The pyramids of Giza," he whispers.

"Let's go," you say. "What should we do with the satchel?"

"We'd better keep it with us," he replies. "We can take turns carrying it."

A few minutes later you're in a taxi speeding toward the pyramids. They loom larger and larger as you near the edge of the city. The taxi drops you off, and you walk the final kilometer over desert sand to Cheops, the first of the great pyramids of Giza.

You're awed by its presence and by the labor that went into stacking the huge mass of stone building blocks. Bruce is as overwhelmed as you are. At last, you think, he's found something bigger than himself.

Turn to page 78.

You're surprised to see your friend Bruce at the courthouse on Monday morning, until you realize that he's also testifying. The hearings go well, as you simply recount what happened when you found the satchel and took it to the police. Bruce backs up your story, although he casts several nasty glances your way for not telling him about the money.

Afterward, everything explodes. The newspapers get hold of the story, and it's splashed all over the front pages. One paper runs a picture of you, with the caption ROBBED BY POLICE. Soon you have reporters camped out on your front lawn, throwing a new batch of questions at you every morning as the case develops.

One day Jean Fahey finally calls you into her office. "It's all going to happen tomorrow," she tells you in her usual sober way. "The grand jury will hand down indictments of several police officers. Even if the charges don't stick, we've established that they haven't found a single clue as to the owner of the satchel. The money is rightfully yours. I'll pick it up at the courthouse tomorrow."

"We've won?" you ask.

"Yes, we've won," she says, allowing herself to smile. You grab her and hug her and do a little dance around her office.

Turn to page 21.

You run downstairs just in time to see Roscoe coming in the front door with a bag of groceries. "Quick!" you say. "A man's got the satchel on the roof—and he has a gun!"

Roscoe drops the groceries onto the floor and rushes out the door, fishing a pistol from the holster underneath his shirt. As you follow, you hear Mrs. Harkley scream. Roscoe's voice commands, "Freeze!"

At the sound of the first gunshot, you take cover in the doorway. "Get him, Roscoe!" Mrs. Harkley shouts. There are more gunshots, steps on the roof, and then a scream. You hear something rolling off the roof, and then West's body comes crashing through the tree in the front yard.

"Good shot, Roscoe!" Mrs. Harkley cries.

You peer out the doorway in time to see Roscoe dragging West's body across the yard and into Mrs. Harkley's station wagon. "Land sakes!" Mrs. Harkley exclaims. "I'm glad I brought Roscoe along with us."

Theresa comes out from hiding behind a bush. "What's he going to do with that man?" she asks.

"Don't you worry about that, honey," Mrs. Harkley replies. "Just thank heaven we're all safe."

Turn to page 62.

"Look at this," you call to Bruce, holding up the satchel. "It's filled with money."

Bruce peers through the branches. "What are you talking about?"

You pick your way out. "I found a briefcase full of money."

You set the satchel down and open it for Bruce to see. He stares blankly for a moment. Then his eyes bug out and his mouth moves, but all he can manage is to stammer, "I can't—I can't believe it." He pulls out a band of bills and flips through it. "They're all hundreds," he says. "There must be a million dollars here."

You look at the money. A crisp green portrait of Benjamin Franklin stares back at you. "I wonder who it belongs to," you muse.

"Who cares?" Bruce answers. "It's ours now."

"No," you say, "we have to try to find the person who lost it."

Bruce looks at you and narrows his eyes. "Are you crazy?" he asks.

"No, I'm not crazy," you reply. "I just think it's the right thing to do."

"Listen," Bruce says with exasperation, "whoever lost this money didn't get it by doing good deeds. Otherwise why would they have stashed it in the bushes?"

"Maybe they stole it from somebody else, and we should try to find the person they stole it from."

"Who's going to be running around with a million dollars in a briefcase?" Bruce says. "It probably belonged to some drug dealer."

Turn to page 52.

A police car screeches to a halt in front of your house, and two officers jump out. "What's going on here?" one of them demands, pulling his gun.

"I caught this guy," Roscoe says, tight-lipped.

"No you didn't," Theresa interrupts. She gestures at you and says, "We did."

The officers look at each other. The first says, "All right, you're all coming down to the station with us."

At the station, you tell a detective the whole story, from finding the money, to having West pull a gun on you, to your capture of him. The detective just shakes his head and says, "Amazing."

After he gets your name and address, he says you can go home. "But be sure you're available for questioning. There's no telling where this will lead. Meanwhile, we're going to keep Roscoe here—that gun of his isn't registered. And West will be under guard at the hospital."

The next morning your exploits are on the front page of the newspaper. Your heroism increases later in the week when the detective calls you in to tell you that he's found out more about West.

"West is who you said he is," the detective tells you. "It's true that he was supporting a counter-revolution in Mombawe. But he was also raising the money by running drugs and guns, and I suspect a lot of it ended up lining his own pockets.

"Unfortunately," he goes on, "that means you won't get to keep the money in the satchel. But you've caught a pretty big fish. There's still a big reward in store for you."

The End

78

A steady stream of camel and horse drivers approaches you, offering you and Bruce rides across the desert to the other pyramids. But you turn them down, deciding you want to go inside Cheops first.

You climb a seemingly endless series of steps through the inside of the pyramid in a low, narrow passage. You're carrying the satchel, and you sweat as the air becomes hot and stuffy. Finally you reach the room in the center of the pyramid where the pharaoh's sarcophagus lies. There's an eerie feeling to this burial chamber surrounded by tons of stone.

You also get a strange feeling from a man in the room. He looks familiar—he's got curly blond hair and is wearing a khaki outfit, as if he's about to embark on a safari. You think maybe he was on the airplane from New York.

You turn to leave, and the man follows you and Bruce back down the passage. Then, all of a sudden, he pushes past Bruce and makes a grab for the satchel. "You've got my money!" he growls.

Bruce jumps the man from behind. You lose your footing, and all three of you go sliding down the passage. People scream as you tumble past them, and soon your threesome turns into an avalanche of bodies careening toward the pyramid's portal.

Turn to page 85.

A few hours later Roscoe returns, exhausted. He just shakes his head when Mrs. Harkley looks at him. By dinnertime he has cleared out of the house.

Things gradually return to normal over the next week. You have a feeling Mrs. Harkley will never forgive you, but you decide not to worry about it.

A few months later, you see Jack West's picture in the newspaper. The caption says the FBI has arrested him for masterminding a drug and weapons smuggling operation. When you read the story, you realize where the money came from. Now it will end up with the U.S. Treasury, instead of in your closet.

The End

80

In the morning you look up "Private Investigators" in the yellow pages. When you find one, you get on your bike and ride down to his office.

The detective rubs his chin after you tell your story and says, "It's sticky business, messing with the police. Normally I wouldn't touch it. I might make an exception—but you'll have to pay for it. Twice my going rate, plus expenses."

"But . . ." you stammer, "I don't have that kind of money. I'll give you a percentage of the money if you get it back."

The detective laughs. "I know you will. But you'll also pay me up front. It's too dicey to do any other way. Sorry, kid."

You resolve to try again. But over and over, you get the same answer: you have to pay up front. Then you start calling lawyers, but their reaction is not much different. "It's just too risky a case," one tells you.

Finally you call Jean Fahey, only to find she's left on vacation. The only thing you can think of is to confront the police head-on.

The next day you march down to the station. Most of the officers recognize you by now, and none of them will give you any answers. Finally you get in to see the captain. He gets out a file, reads through it, and tells you, "I'm sorry. We've closed that case. There's nothing more we can do."

"But where's the satchel? Don't I get it back?"

"Sorry, I can't answer that. Department security. Now if you'll excuse me, I have work to do."

That's the most you ever find out.

The End

"No," you say, "but we could describe the satchel, without saying what was inside. The caller would have to identify the contents."

"I guess that's right," Mrs. Harkley admits. Then her face brightens. "I imagine there will be quite a reward."

You run upstairs and inspect the satchel carefully so that you can write a description. You find a faded set of initials, O.K.N., in gold letters on the side of the case. Mrs. Harkley insists on helping you write the want ad. "I'll call it in first thing in the morning," she says.

That night your sleep is restless. You're excited and nervous about the money and about finding the owner. You wonder who it is.

Turn to page 115.

"All right," you say to Bruce. "Let's do it. Let's go to Egypt and see the pyramids."

"Yeah!" Bruce responds. "We can leave right away. Do you have a passport?"

"My parents made me get one last year," you say. "But don't we need more time to get ready?"

"What for?" Bruce replies. "We can buy whatever we need along the way."

"I guess so. And we can send postcards home to tell people not to worry about us."

You go home feeling a thrill in your stomach. You've never done anything this crazy. But you figure if you're going to live dangerously, Bruce is the person to do it with.

After dinner you grab your passport and toothbrush, slip out of the house, and meet Bruce at the corner. He's already called a taxi to take you to the airport.

You and Bruce manage to get on a night flight to New York and book two first-class seats on a plane out of New York for Cairo.

Twenty-four hours later, exhausted and excited, you land at Cairo International Airport. But your feeling soon changes when you reach customs and find that you're required to declare all your currency.

"What are we going to do?" you ask Bruce.

"Fake it," he says. "And if that doesn't work, we'll use the old-fashioned way—we'll bribe them."

Turn to page 110.

84

You shake your head at Bill. You'd rather not tell all these people about the money. It's too risky to let so many people in on it. "Let's just forget it," you say, and look away.

Bill shrugs and changes the subject. Pretty soon people start yawning and decide it's time to sneak back into their bunks. "You can hide with me," Bill says. "I've got a sleeping bag you can use."

In the morning you head back home on the bus. Mrs. Harkley is furious at you for going away without telling her. "I was worried sick!" she scolds you. "What would I tell your parents if something happened to you? You're grounded for a week!"

You figure you'll have to obey her and not cause any more trouble. But you feel better, knowing that in a week you'll be able to start spending your money.

The time passes slowly, but finally the end of the week comes. The morning of the following day you wake up early, eager to go down to the mall and shop.

Turn to page 7.

Somehow you manage to keep hold of the satchel, and when you hit bottom, you feel Bruce pulling you up out of the tangle. The two of you dash away from the pyramid, looking for a way to escape. At one of the underground burial temples next to the pyramid, you spot a tunnel leading into the rock. The entrance is blocked by steel bars, but a gap between two of the bars looks just wide enough for the two of you to slip through.

Meanwhile, a camel driver approaches, asking if you want a ride. Glancing back at the pyramid, you see the man in the khaki outfit shaking himself off and looking around for you.

If you escape into the tunnel, turn to page 96.

If you escape by camel, turn to page 98.

When you and Bruce reach the top of the ladder, a man pulls you inside the helicopter. He's tall and impressive looking, even though he's dressed as a tourist. He introduces himself as Josef and another man in the helicopter as Nelson.

The helicopter hovers over the Nile. Josef points down at the man who's been chasing you, and you see he is being handcuffed and taken aboard an Egyptian police boat. The pilot banks the helicopter and heads back toward Cairo.

You finally get up the nerve to ask, "What's going on here?"

"We've just captured a terrorist," Nelson says. He and Josef chuckle together. "You probably have no idea who that man in the boat was. His name is Jack West, and he is trying to overthrow the government of our country."

"What country is that?" Bruce asks.

"Mombawe," Nelson answers. Seeing your blank look, he goes on, "It's a small country to the south of here. I wish more Americans knew about it. Maybe they would stop people like Jack West from carrying out his schemes."

Go on to the next page.

"A few years ago," Josef picks up, "Mombawe was ruled by one man and his cronies. They were so cruel and greedy that finally one day people could take it no more. They rose up and overthrew him. Of course, his henchmen did not want to lose power, so they started a counterrevolutionary guerrilla movement.

"Jack West is on the side of the guerrillas. He doesn't like the way our new government is acting. We do certain things differently than you do in your country. There are a handful of people like West who feel it is their right to tell us how to live. They want to force us to believe in their way of life."

Turn to page 108.

Bruce shines the flashlight over the edge. "I can't tell what's down there. But there are steps cut in the rock."

"Well," you reason, "we can't go back the way we came."

"I'll go first," Bruce says. "Then you can drop the satchel to me and come down yourself."

Bruce puts the flashlight between his teeth and carefully lowers himself over the edge. You watch the light get smaller and smaller as he climbs down. Finally he calls, "Okay, let it drop."

You hold the satchel out over the edge and let go. It takes a couple of seconds to thunk at the bottom. "Got it," Bruce says. "Come on down. I'm in some kind of chamber."

You slide over the edge, feeling for the stone steps in the dark. Your foot finds one, and you gingerly allow your weight to rest on it. Then you find another one for your other foot, and one for your hand. You slowly descend to the chamber below, concentrating so hard on each step as it comes that you don't have time to get scared.

"Good work," Bruce says as you find level ground again. The air is dank and stale. It feels cold after the heat outside.

He turns and shines the light into the chamber.

"A sarcophagus!" you gasp.

Warily, you and Bruce approach the black marble coffin. The top is off. Bruce shines the light in. Staring up at you is the frozen grimace of a half-unwrapped mummy!

Turn to page 58.

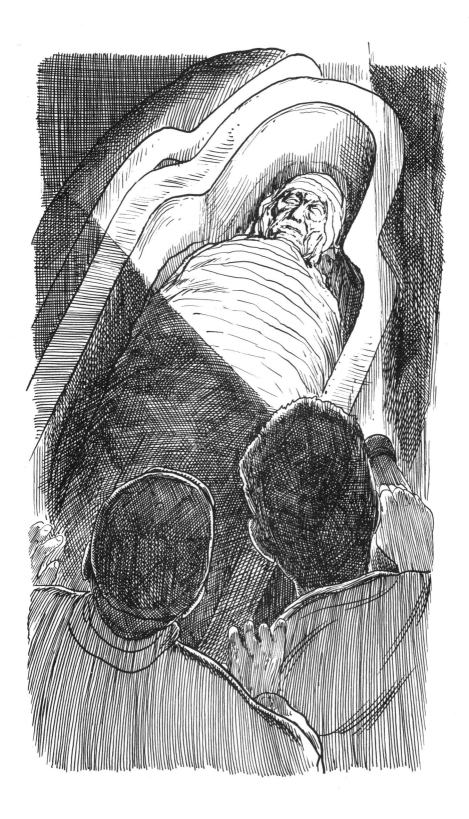

90

After you have spent a miserable night in jail, a man from the U.S. Consulate arrives to spring you. He takes you back to his office and sits you down.

Soon another man arrives. "I'm Louis B. Jordan," he says, sitting down behind the desk. "You're in some fairly serious trouble. First of all, there is the matter of attempting to bribe an officer of the Egyptian Civil Guard. Now, this is not unheard of. But it must be done correctly. Do you know what *baksheesh* is?"

You and Bruce shake your heads.

"Literally speaking, it's a gift. It can be the money you give to a beggar, or a tip you give to someone who performs a service. It can also be what we would call a bribe. But that is a very delicate art. You must develop a relationship with the person, do a kind of dance, before you begin to negotiate. All of this is done very subtly, through hints. From what I understand, your methods were, shall we say, crude."

Jordan pauses to light a cigar. "So much for your first mistake. However, it leads to a much bigger question: where in heaven's name did you get all that money?"

Turn to page 97.

You step aside, letting Bruce into the bushes, and go back to the vacant lot, trying to act nonchalant. But your heart sinks when Bruce cries, "Hey, look what I found! Hey, it's full of money!"

You stand paralyzed, unable to respond. Bruce comes tromping out of the bushes, holding the satchel. "I'm rich! I'm rich! Look at this!"

You finally manage to speak. "I know, Bruce. I already saw it."

Bruce guffaws. "Sure you did. And you just left it there because you didn't need it."

"I really did see it first, Bruce."

"Oh, and you weren't going to tell me about it. I get it," Bruce says. "Well, even if you did see it, which I doubt, you don't deserve to have it. "

"I'll split it with you," you plead.

"Gee thanks," Bruce mocks. "I hate to tell you, but it's not up to you. But luckily I'm a nice guy, and I'm going to share some of it with you." He pulls a few bundles of bills from the satchel and throws them at your feet. "There you go, ingrate."

Bruce starts to walk away. You stare down at the money, transfixed. Knowing you have no chance to get the satchel away from Bruce by force, you just pick up the money and go home.

That night, the more you think about what happened, the madder you get. You get up bright and early the next morning and go straight to Bruce's house. His mother answers the doorbell. Her eyes are red. Before you can say anything, she says, "Bruce has run away again. But this time he left a note. He's never coming back."

Turn to page 31.

"I don't know," you say. "I'll have to think about it. Why don't you leave your telephone number and—"

Suddenly a snub-nosed pistol is in West's hand. "I've played games long enough with you, kid," he snarls. "Now let's go get the satchel."

You can see he's not fooling around. You turn and walk very carefully up the stairs into your room, with West close behind. As you pull out the satchel, he grabs it from you. Then he glares at you and fingers the pistol, as if he's trying to decide what to do with you.

At that moment you hear a car pull into the driveway. West hears it, too. "Who is that?" he demands.

"Mrs. Harkley," you answer. "And her nephew Roscoe."

West hesitates for only a second before opening your window and climbing out onto the ledge. You watch as he stands up on the ledge and pulls himself onto the roof. Downstairs, you hear the key in the door. Should you go after West yourself? Or should you let Roscoe handle it?

If you tell Roscoe that West is on the roof, turn to page 74.

If you go out the window after West, turn to page 57.

You tell them how you found the satchel in a vacant lot, hidden in the bushes.

"You just *found* it there," the detective says skeptically. You nod.

The detective looks over at the other policemen in the room. He takes a deep breath and says, "You must understand this looks pretty suspicious. Here you walk into a bank with a satchel full of money, you're covered with bruises, you have blood all over your face, your clothes are torn to shreds—and you say you just *found* some money. Now, if you were me, what would you think?"

"But I can explain," you answer quickly, proceeding to tell them about your fight with Bruce.

The detective nods as you speak. When you're done, he dispatches an officer to bring Bruce down to the station. "We'll check out your story," he says. "But even if your friend can confirm it, we'll have to hold you in custody until we find out exactly where the money came from, and whether a crime was committed." Seeing the frightened look on your face, he adds, "It won't be so bad. The first thing we need to do is get a doctor to fix up those cuts."

Two weeks later you're back home, cleared of any wrongdoing, but also of any claim to the money. The detective tells you it's been funneled to the "proper channels." You never do find out where it came from or where it went.

Bruce calls the next day. "I knew you were a dweeb," he says.

The End

You watch as Bruce starts pulling money out of the satchel. "There's no problem," he says, making a wiping motion with his hand. "We are very generous." He pulls some bills from the satchel and flips them onto the desk. "No problems, no problems," he chants lightly.

You sneak a glance at the officer, who looks aghast. "What's the matter?" Bruce asks. "That's not enough?" He keeps dropping money onto the desk.

Looking back at the officer, you now realize he is deeply offended. He stands up and says in a formal manner, "I must tell you that you are under arrest for attempting to bribe an officer of the civil guard." He gestures to the guards, who take each of you by an elbow.

"What is this briefcase?" the officer asks coldly.

"Oh it's nothing, nothing," Bruce stammers.

The officer directs a guard to bring him the satchel, which he opens. Shock registers on his face for a moment, then he asks, "Did you declare this currency at customs?"

Bruce's hesitation is all he needs. "I am confiscating this until the matter can be investigated," the officer says, and waves you away. With that, you're taken down to the police station.

Turn to page 90.

96

"This way!" you say, grabbing Bruce's sleeve. You lead him down a ramp to the barred entrance to the tunnel. "I doubt he'll be able to follow us here," you say, squeezing through the gap in the bars.

"I doubt he'd want to," Bruce replies, peering in at the blackness in front of you. "I'm glad I bought a flashlight at the hotel."

"Come on," you say. "We have to get out of sight, in case he saw us come down here."

Bruce switches on the flashlight, and you venture down the rock corridor. You haven't gone very far before you hear a man yelling in at you, "Hey, come back here! I won't hurt you, I promise. I just want to talk. That's my satchel you've got!"

Bruce turns off the flashlight. You wait in silence. The man rattles the bars. "Get back here, you kids," he screams. "You'll be sorry. This is serious business! That's not your money! I work for the company!"

"What company?" Bruce whispers.

You shrug. "Let's go." You and Bruce move silently down the tunnel in darkness until you can no longer hear the man. Something brushes by your face, then a lot of things brush past you in a flutter of high-pitched squeaks.

"Bats!" Bruce hisses. You crouch and wait for the flurry of bats to pass. Bruce turns the flashlight on again, and not a moment too soon. Six feet in front of you is a sheer drop-off.

Turn to page 88.

Seeing little choice, you tell Jordan how you found the satchel and decided to come to see the pyramids. Jordan puffs and nods for a few minutes and then says, "Obviously, we'll have to conduct a full investigation. But for the time being, I'm willing to buy your story. Your actions are not those of criminals, or indeed of people who know how to handle money in any way.

"I'll have to turn the money over to the Department of Treasury," Jordan continues. "In the meantime, I'm afraid we'll have to put you on a plane back to the United States."

You and Bruce have a long flight ahead—in economy class.

The End

You pull a handful of Egyptian pounds from your pocket, hand them to the camel driver, and say, "Let's go!"

"*Yela,*" the driver says, repeating your command in Arabic. He loads Bruce up onto the saddle between the humps of one of the camels, then helps you onto the other. He jumps onto his camel, applies the whip, and you're off. The camels gallop in a weird, exaggerated galumphing motion that tosses you high in the air with each stride. It's probably the most painful ride you've ever had, but that doesn't matter at the moment.

You glance back, only to see that the man who tried to grab the satchel is galloping after you on horseback. "Faster!" you shout to the driver. "*Yela! Yela!*" the driver cries, whipping his camel.

You gallop past the last pyramid, out into the Egyptian desert. But the man on horseback is gaining on you. You won't be able to outrun him on a camel, and in the open desert there's nowhere to hide. You point back to the man chasing you and yell to the driver, "We must escape him."

"You can pay?" the driver yells back. You nod vigorously. He wheels to the left and leads you back toward the green strip of civilization along the banks of the Nile. Before long a group of men lounging alongside two old army jeeps comes into view. The camel driver goes on ahead and yells something to them in Arabic. By the time you get there, one of the jeeps is running.

Go on to the next page.

The driver talks quickly to the man in the jeep. As you and Bruce dismount, the camel driver turns to you and says, "Hamid will take you, if you pay in advance."

You jump into the jeep and start peeling hundred-pound notes from your wad, handing them to Hamid. He nods each time you hand him one, but after five you stop, saying, "That's all."

Hamid looks stony faced at you. Meanwhile, the man in the khaki outfit is approaching fast on his horse. "Stop!" he cries as he rides up in a cloud of dust.

Turn to page 66.

You grab Bruce's hand, silently restraining him from bribing the officer. You look at the officer and wonder if that's a twinkle you see in his eye.

"Yes, our countries have become friends," you say to the officer.

"Yes, and America has helped us to develop our economy," the officer responds, eyeing the satchel.

Maybe now is the time to make your move. "We would like to help your economy develop. Perhaps you have established a fund for this?"

The officer tugs on his mustache. "Yes, in fact, we do have such a fund. Would you like to make a contribution?"

"Why yes, we would," you reply.

"Ahem, well, I can take your contribution myself. I will see that it gets to the correct bureau."

"I would appreciate that very much," you say. You pull a bundle of bills from the satchel and set it on his desk. The officer regards them, saying nothing. You put another bundle of bills on the desk. You wait. He waits. You put one more bundle on the desk. He chews his mustache and looks at his watch. You add another bundle, clap the satchel shut, and stand up.

The officer regards you and then the money on the desk. "You Americans are very generous," he murmurs. He breaks into a smile. "Thank you very much for your contribution." He stands to shake your hand, then gestures to one of the guards behind you. "Mustafa, see these fine people to the door."

Turn to page 11.

102

Leaning on your elbows, you tilt your head back and use your T-shirt to stop your nosebleed. Finally you get to your feet. A wave of dizziness hits you. You have to lie down again until it passes.

You head back into the bushes for the satchel, lug it out, and sit down. When you start pulling the money out, you find it's wrapped up in neat bundles of hundred-dollar bills. You pull out bundle after bundle in amazement. The money feels weird—you can't believe it's real. You wonder where it came from. The serial numbers aren't in order, and the bills aren't new.

You close the satchel, realizing you don't want to stay in the vacant lot in case Bruce comes back.

You pick the satchel up, surprised to find it's very heavy. Where should you take it? you wonder. Should you keep it for yourself or try to find out who it belongs to? You could go straight to the bank and deposit it right now, or you could take it home and think it over.

If you head for the bank, turn to page 12.

If you go home, turn to page 14.

A week goes by before you hear from Sergeant Winooski. "We've been searching high and low," she tells you on the phone, "but we can't figure out where the money came from. But we'll keep looking, and I'll let you know the minute anything happens."

Another week goes by before Sergeant Winooski calls again. She sounds cautious and worried. "There have been some bureaucratic foul-ups in regard to your money," she tells you. "I can't really go into it now, but I'm not sure what's happening. My superiors have taken it out of my hands and won't give me a straight answer about what they're doing with the satchel. Just try to sit tight," she says before hanging up.

Sixteen days later you've heard nothing more from Sergeant Winooski. The thirty-day waiting period is up. Late in the afternoon, you decide to go down to the station.

Sergeant Winooski looks startled when you walk into her office. "Oh, hello," she says. "I didn't expect to see you here."

"I just thought I'd check on the satchel," you say, trying to sound unconcerned.

"I'm sorry I haven't gotten back to you about that." She lowers her voice. "The truth is, there are some odd things happening around here. I can't really talk about it now—why don't you come tomorrow, first thing in the morning?"

Suddenly the sergeant's eyes show fear as she looks up at the door. You turn to see a captain glaring at her from the hallway.

Turn to page 46.

You recognize the voice as Bruce's. Behind him are his friends Kelly and Roger. Turning to face him, you say, "We're checking out your fort."

"Oh, yeah?" he replies. "Who said you could?"

Theresa breaks in before you can answer. "You two better not get going again," she says. "There are more important things to talk about."

"Like what?" Kelly demands, hands on her hips.

"Like money. I have all this money, and we're going to spend it," you say, trying not to sound cocky. "That's where the fort comes in. I want to build a secret place where we can keep our stuff. It'll be like a clubhouse."

"We who?" Bruce asks, his lip curled.

"You, me, Theresa . . . whoever," you answer. "There's enough for everybody."

"I'm going to buy a horse," Theresa puts in, "and build a stall for it."

"Where'd this money come from?" Roger asks.

"I just found it," you respond. "I can't tell you any more. You'll just have to take my word for it."

Bruce and his two friends stare at you, trying to take in what you're saying. Bruce narrows his eyes. "Is this some kind of trick?"

"No," you say, looking straight at him.

After a few moments, Bruce smiles and sticks his hand out. You shake it.

Turn to page 26.

"Where's the felucca?" you ask Hamid.

"I'll take you," he says, swinging the jeep in a sharp turn toward the river. With a couple more turns, you find yourselves at a dock where several simple sailboats are moored. You and Bruce jump onto one of the feluccas. Hamid speaks quickly to the captain and then pushes you off, just as the man in the khaki outfit pulls up in his jeep.

The single sail of the felucca billows out, and soon you're moving at a good clip up the Nile. But now the captain wants to take care of business— he gestures that you should pay him. "I do this as a favor, for my friend Hamid," he says. You peel off several pound notes, and he seems satisfied.

But, looking downriver, you find that the news is bad. Somehow your pursuer has gotten hold of a motorboat, and he's roaring up the river after you. The felucca captain sees him, too, and holds out his hands, saying, "What can I do?"

Turn to page 107.

"Maybe we should try to swim for it," you say, forgetting about Bruce.

"No," the captain says, wagging his finger. "Crocodiles."

At that moment a helicopter swoops down out of nowhere over the felucca. Bruce looks stricken. "I give up," he mutters.

The helicopter comes in for another pass, slowing down as it hovers above you. The captain takes down the sail as a ladder is lowered from the helicopter. Then you see that someone from above is firing a rifle at the man in the motorboat, forcing him to keep his distance.

"What do we have to lose?" you say to Bruce, grabbing the ladder.

Turn to page 86.

"West is helping the guerrillas because he feels threatened by our government," Josef goes on. "But he's also in it for the money. He smuggles drugs and weapons—that's where most of that money in the satchel you have came from. He tells those who support him in your country that it's going to be used to buy supplies. But you can bet a good chunk of it ends up in his pocket. We're lucky the Egyptian army agreed to loan us this helicopter."

The helicopter begins to descend to an Egyptian military base. "So why did you save us?" you ask.

Josef looks at you for a second. "Why not?" he says with a shrug. "You're innocent people. We wanted to catch West."

"We've been tracking him for a long time," Nelson adds. "He ditched the money when he figured out we were onto him. Ever since then, he's been chasing you, and we've been chasing him."

"So I suppose you want the money?" Bruce blurts out.

Josef shrugs again. "Of course, we would not mind. That money could fund many development projects for people in Mombawe—people who have no clean water, no fertilizer, no money to buy seeds. . . . But it is yours. You acted heroically to keep it from West. You do what you want with it."

Turn to page 24.

At dinner, you only mention that you had a fight with Bruce. You feel funny not telling your sister Theresa, or Mrs. Harkley, about the money. You also feel a little guilty, as if you've just embarked on a life of crime and deception.

After you've washed the dishes, you go up to your room and putter about. But you can't concentrate on anything. You're thinking too much about the money and what to do with it.

You're rich now. You look at yourself in the mirror, trying to see a difference. You look the same. It's disappointing—you thought when something like this happened you'd suddenly become a totally different person. But you don't feel any different, except that you know there's a briefcase full of money in your closet.

Maybe once you start spending it, things will change. You'll change. It *has* to change your life somehow—for starters, you can buy whatever you want. You fall asleep thinking of all the things you may soon own.

When you wake up in the morning, you wonder if you do want to keep the money all to yourself. Your best friend, Bill, is at summer camp in the mountains. You could take a taxi up there to visit him. Or would you rather take the taxi downtown to the shopping mall and start buying things?

If you go to the shopping mall, turn to page 7.

If you go to visit Bill at summer camp, turn to page 32.

Luck, however, seems to be on your side. When your turn comes, the customs agent glances at your passport, stamps it, and lets you through. You proceed to the exchange window, where you change two bundles of bills into Egyptian pounds. Then you look for a taxi to take you into the city.

Cairo is a shock to you at first. It's crowded, dirty, and noisy—like nothing you've ever seen before. The taxi drives at breakneck speed, honking constantly at the cars, pedestrians, carts, chickens, sheep, and even herds of goats that crowd the road. Everything seems to be covered with a layer of brown desert dust. The city is full of unfamiliar sounds and smells, such as the call to prayer from the mosques or the sharp odors of turmeric and other spices.

Your ride ends in front of the Nile Hilton in Tahrir Square, the modern hub of Cairo. "The Hilton's too boring. Let's go to the Queen Cleopatra," you say to Bruce, pointing at a neon sign advertising the hotel. Twenty minutes later, you're asleep in your room at the Queen Cleopatra.

Turn to page 71.

112

"Take us into the desert, Hamid," you direct. "Maybe we can lose this guy there."

Hamid swerves sharply, and soon you're striking out across the open desert, leaving civilization behind. But looking back, you also realize you're leaving tracks.

You ask Hamid if he can go faster. "My foot is on the floor," he replies dryly.

"This isn't working," Bruce informs you. "No matter how fast we go, that guy can still follow our tracks."

"What can we do?" you say. "It's too late to turn back."

Three hours go by, in which you continue to blaze into the desert, without putting much distance between you and your pursuer. Then, all of a sudden, your jeep coughs, sputters, and comes to a dead stop. Hamid sighs and turns to you. "Out of gas," he says simply.

There's nowhere to hide in the desert. You have no choice but to await being caught. The man spins to a halt behind you, jumps out of his jeep, trains a gun on you, and says, "All right, hand it over."

You toss the satchel at his feet. He picks it up and retreats to the jeep. "Hey," Bruce calls to him, "now that you've got what you want, how about giving us a hand?"

The man just laughs, making a U-turn.

"What now?" you say to Hamid.

"Maybe we get lucky and a caravan comes along," he says with seeming indifference. "But most likely, we die of thirst."

The End

"I can't do it," you say to Bruce. "It feels wrong to take money we haven't earned. I'm going to turn it in to the police."

"Now hold on a second," Bruce responds. "You can take your half to the police, but I'm going to keep my half for myself."

"Since when do you get half?"

"Well, we found it together, didn't we? You never would have found it if I hadn't thrown the ball into the bushes."

"I think we should take it all to the police."

"No way," Bruce says. "You can't tell me what to do with my half."

You stand facing each other, neither one moving. You can see that you're not going to be able to get Bruce to turn any money in to the police. Since he's bigger than you, you don't have much choice but to split it and just turn in your half.

Turn to page 8.

A tiny click wakes you in the middle of the night. Your eyes pop open, and immediately you sense someone in the room. As your eyes adjust to the darkness, you make out a shape looming in the doorway. Your first thought is that it's a burglar. You freeze, closing your eyes and trying to make your breathing regular so the intruder will think you're asleep. But your mind is racing. You can't believe your bad luck—the very night you find a briefcase full of money, a thief comes into your room!

The shape moves toward your closet. The thought of losing the money is too much for you to bear. A baseball bat is hidden under your bed. You get ready to leap out of bed, grab the bat, and knock the burglar over the head. But at the last moment you have second thoughts. Is it worth risking your life, even for a million dollars?

If you jump out of bed and grab the bat, turn to page 70.

If you continue to pretend you're asleep, turn to page 35.

116

"Watch what you're doing, buster," you snap at Bruce, shoving him away from you.

He pushes you in the chest, retorting, "I *told* you to keep your hands *offa* me!"

"Watch it, fatso!" you say, pushing back.

Bruce's eyes light up in anger. You knew this would happen. His weight is one thing Bruce is really sensitive about. He slaps your head. You lunge at him, butting his chest and pummeling his belly. He wrestles you to the ground. Sharp branches tear at your clothes and skin. You grapple together, rolling one over the other through the bushes until you come out on open ground.

You give him a good fight, but Bruce's greater size and weight slowly begin to win out. You find yourself pinned to the ground, exhausted, with Bruce sitting on your back, pushing your face into the dirt. "That'll teach you, you little dweeb," he crows. "Eat dirt. Are you a little dweeb?"

You say nothing, determined to hold out. Bruce twists your hair and pushes your face harder into the ground. "Are you a little dweeb?" he taunts. You can barely breathe.

Then you remind yourself of the purpose of the whole fight. "I'm a little dweeb," you say, trying to sound defeated.

Turn to page 6.

You find it difficult to speak. But you don't need to, because Bruce goes on, "You know what else they say: there's no such thing as a free lunch. But today I'll make an exception. You can come to my club for lunch."

You look at Theresa and shrug. "Why not?"

Theresa agrees, and Bruce claps you on the back. "Fabulous. Now, tell me what you've been up to."

You tell him a little about school and the other things you've been doing until he interrupts and says, "Enough about you, let's talk about me."

For the rest of the ride, and on through the lunch at his club, Bruce regales you with tales of his life and his possessions: his house in Hawaii, his house in Bermuda, his house in London, the art in his houses, his cars, his power meetings, his quarterly profits, his season tickets, his "babes." By the end of lunch, you're bored to death with it and wonder if he isn't a little bit, too.

Bruce checks his watch. "Well, gotta make some more dough," he says. "Here's some money for a taxi home."

"That's all right," you say, pushing his hand away.

You and Theresa watch as his limo speeds off. "Bruce really seems to have it all," Theresa says.

"There but for Fortune," you muse, "go I."

The End

ABOUT THE AUTHOR

JAY LEIBOLD was born in Denver, Colo., and now lives in San Francisco. This is his fourteenth book in the Choose Your Own Adventure series. Recent titles include *Surf Monkeys,* and *The Search for Aladdin's Lamp. Ninja Cyborg* is the fourth ninja book he's done. The first three are *Secret of the Ninja, Return of the Ninja,* and *The Lost Ninja.*

Mr. Leibold is also the author of the Dojo Rats series, published by Bantam Books, under the pen name James Raven.

ABOUT THE ILLUSTRATOR

RON WING is a cartoonist and illustrator who has contribued to many publications. His Choose Your Own Adventure credits include *You Are a Millionaire, Skateboard Champion, The Island of Time, Vampire Invaders, Outlaw Gulch, The Forgotten Planet,* and *Everest Adventure!* Ron Wing lives and works in Benton, Pennsylvania.